Rex

Ursula Dubosarsky
Illustrated by David Mackintosh

SCHOLASTIC INC.

New York Toronto London Auckland Sydney
Mexico City New Delhi Hong Kong Buenos Aires

For the fabulous Shrubb family—U.D. • For Ruby Middleton and Tierry D'Actil—D.M.

ISBN-13: 978-0-545-03783-9
ISBN-10: 0-545-03783-2

Text copyright © 2005 by Ursula Dubosarsky
Illustrations copyright © 2005 by David Mackintosh

12 11 10 9 8 7 6 5 4 3 2 1   7 8 9 10 11/0

Printed in the U.S.A.   08
First Scholastic printing, September 2007

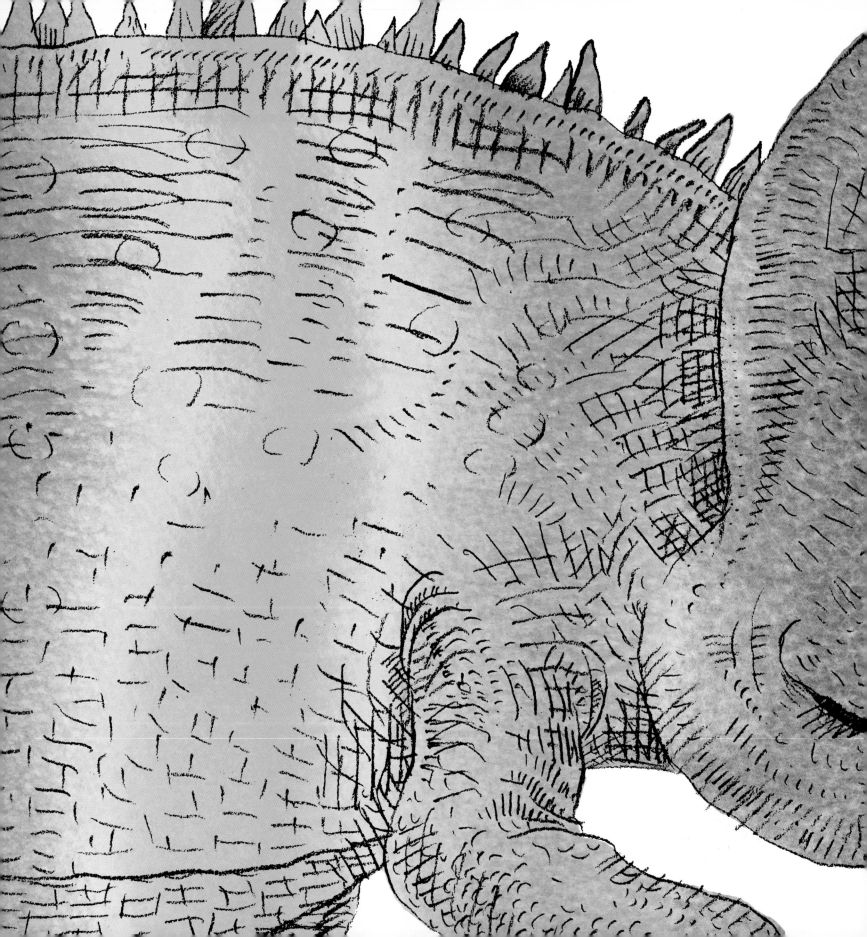

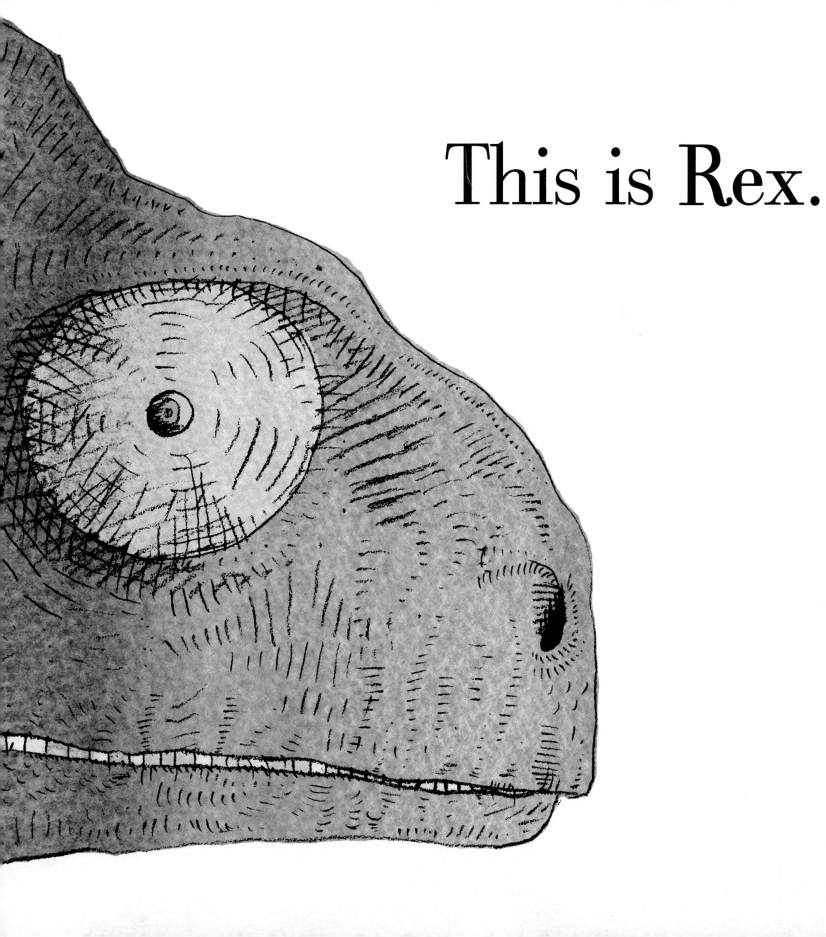

This is Rex.

Rex is our class pet.

Every day, someone
gets to take Rex home.

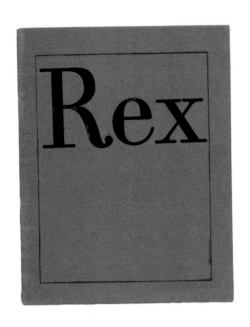  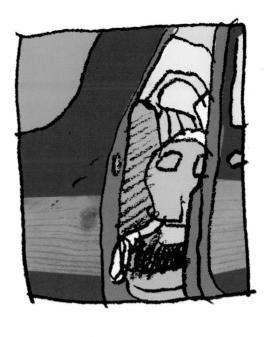

You take Rex home with a special book.

  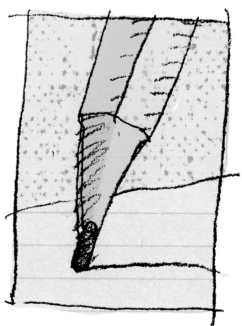

In the special book, you write
all the things Rex did on his visit.

If you can't
write,

...you can
draw a picture.

On Monday, Rex went home with Jai.

Jai has a swimming pool.
Rex went for a swim.

Lucky he can float.

On Tuesday, Hilary took Rex home.
Hilary lives in a big apartment building.

Rex fell out
the window.

He was a bit surprised,
but at least nobody
was underneath.

On Wednesday, Sam took Rex home.
Rex helped Sam's mom in the shop.

Some of the customers got scared. Rex is used to that.

On Thursday, Amy took Rex home.

Amy has a little brother.

He dressed Rex up in Malibu Barbie's clothes.
It's a good thing Rex has a sense of humor.

Now it's Friday.
At last it's my turn!

I'm lucky. I can have Rex for the whole weekend.
I wonder what I will do with Rex?

Maybe we will go to the movies.
What sort of movie would Rex like?

Or to a restaurant.
Would Rex like a giant hamburger?

Maybe we will hide behind
the door and jump out
when someone goes by.

AAAAAAA AAAAAAA AAGGGGH HHH!

Then, when we are tired, we will snuggle up under the blankets and go to sleep.

I wonder if Rex snores?

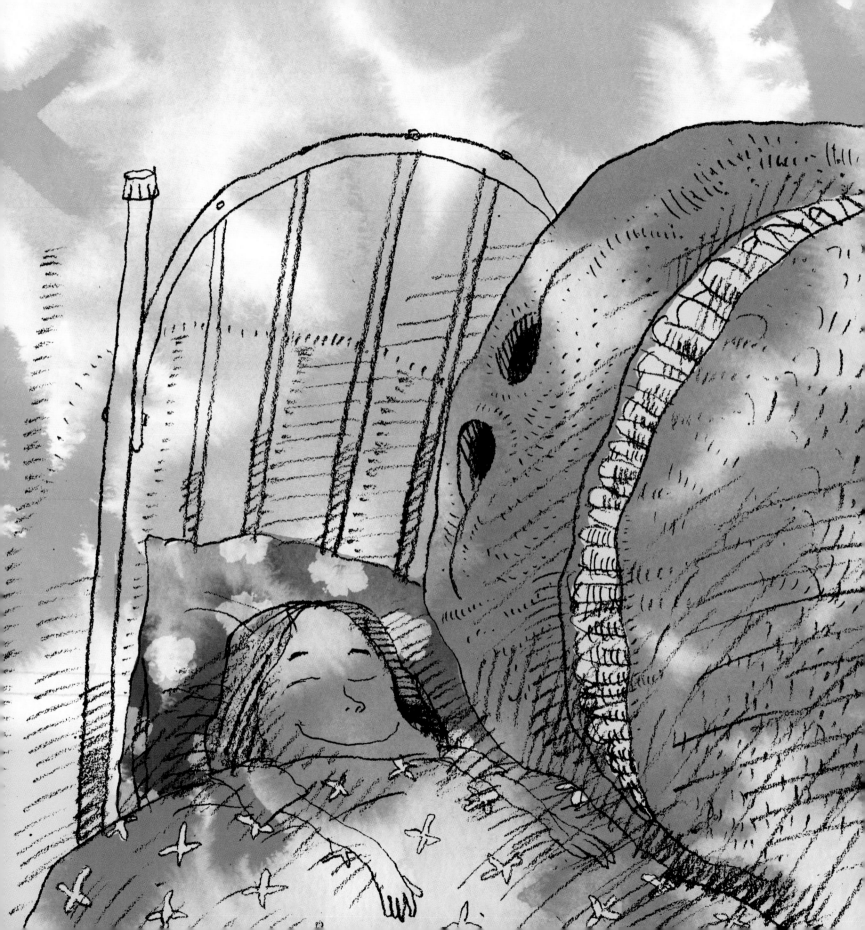

I love Rex.
What would *you* do if Rex came to visit *you*?